A Note to Parents

Dorling Kindersley Classic Readers is a compelling new program for beginning readers, designed in conjunction with leading literacy experts, including Dr. Linda Gambrell, President of the National Reading Conference and past board member of the International Reading Association.

Beautiful illustrations and superb full-color photographs combine with engaging, easy-to-read stories to offer a fresh approach to each subject in the series. Each *Dorling Kindersley Classic Reader* is guaranteed to capture a child's interest while developing his or her reading skills, general knowledge, and love of reading.

The four levels of *Dorling Kindersley Classic Readers* are aimed at different reading abilities, enabling you to choose the books that are exactly right for your children:

Level 1, for **Preschool to Grade 1**
Level 2, for **Grades 1 to 3**
Level 3, for **Grades 2 and 3**
Level 4, for **Grades 2 to 4**

The "normal" age at which a child begins to read can be anywhere from three to eight years old, so these levels are intended only as a general guideline.

No matter which level you select, you can be sure that you are helping your child learn to read, then read to learn!

A Dorling Kindersley Book
www.dk.com

Created by Leapfrog Press Ltd

Project Editor Caryn Jenner
Art Editor Catherine Goldsmith

For Dorling Kindersley
Senior Editor Marie Greenwood
Managing Art Editor Jacquie Gulliver
Managing Editor Joanna Devereux
Production Chris Avgherinos
Picture Researcher Liz Moore
Cover Design Margherita Gianni

Reading Consultant
Linda B. Gambrell, Ph.D.

First American edition, 2000
2 4 6 8 10 9 7 5 3 1

Published in the United States by Dorling Kindersley
Publishing, Inc.
95 Madison Avenue, New York, New York 10016

Dorling Kindersley Classic Readers™ is a trademark
of Dorling Kindersley Limited, London.

A catalog record is available from the Library of Congress.

ISBN 0-7894-5388-6

The publisher would like to thank the following for their kind
permission to reproduce their photographs:
Key: t=top, a=above, b=below, c=center

The publisher would like to thank the following:
Key: a = above, b = below, c = centre,´r = right, l = left.
Bridgeman Art Library: 31b, 32c, 38t, 41t,43t; Mary Evans Picture
Library: 14t, 25t, 26t, 32t, 34b, 35t, 36b, 37t, 39t 40t, 43t,
46t, 47t; Kobal: 5t; Bob Langrish: 5b, 19rc,25b, 45b.

Additional photography by: Andy Crawford, Kit Houghton,
Bob Langrish, Ray Moller, Norfolk Rural Life/Geoff Brightling,
Matthew Ward, Jerry Young

Colour reproduction by Colourscan, Singapore
Printed and bound in Belgium by Proost

Contents

DK CLASSIC READERS

Level **4** GRADES 2-4

BLACK BEAUTY

THE GREATEST HORSE STORY EVER TOLD

By Anna Sewell

Adapted by Caryn Jenner

Illustrated by
Victor Ambrus

DK

Dorling Kindersley
www.dk.com

A horse's life story

Anna Sewell's story of a horse, *Black Beauty,* was published in 1877. Cars were not yet invented, so people in Victorian England depended on horses for everyday transportation.

Horses were working animals, not pets, and they were often badly treated. Anna Sewell wrote her book to encourage people to be kinder to horses and other animals.

The title page of the first copies of *Black Beauty* called the book, "the autobiography of a horse, translated from the original equine (ek-wine)".

Of course, Anna Sewell did not really translate the story from horse language. She told Black Beauty's story from his point of view, describing a noble animal's thoughts and feelings.

Working horses
Victorian people used horses like we use machines – to move heavy goods, to work on farms, and for all sorts of transportation.

Riding crop

Riding gloves

Audience
Anna wrote the story for those who worked with horses – grooms, stablehands, and drivers – rather than children.

Beauty's powerful voice helped to change people's attitudes toward animal welfare in Sewell's time.

It continues to do so today. *Black Beauty* remains one of the most popular stories of all time for adults and children.

Film stars
Beauty, Ginger, and Merrylegs in a 1994 movie of *Black Beauty*.

A foal is born

On the farm where I was born there was a large and pleasant meadow. My master was a kind man, and I liked the farm very much.

For the first few weeks of my life, I drank only my mother's milk. As soon as I was old enough to eat grass, my mother went back to work, while I stayed in the meadow with the other colts. We had great fun racing around and playing games in our meadow!

One day when my mother came home, she saw us kicking around.

Newborn foal
A foal is born with a soft, downy coat. Within an hour after birth, the foal can stand up.

Two weeks
A foal gains strength from feeding on its mother's milk.

"Please don't kick, even in play," she told me. "I want you to grow up to be a good and gentle horse who always does his work well."

My mother was a very wise horse and I have never forgotten her advice.

Eight weeks
By eight weeks old, a foal can eat grass, as well as drink its mother's milk.

Four months
By four months old, the foal is strong and sturdy and its coat is shiny.

Bridle

Reins

Bridle
A rider guides
a horse using
reins attached
to a bridle.

Saddle

Stirrup

Saddle
A rider sits in a
saddle with his
feet in stirrups.

I grew into a fine horse, with a
soft black coat and a pretty white
star on my forehead.

When I was four years old,
my master decided it was time to
break me in. I could no longer jump
for joy or lie down to rest whenever
I wanted.

I learned to wear a bridle and
a saddle. One morning, my master
patted me gently. Then he climbed
into the saddle and rode me around
the meadow. It felt quite peculiar to
have a person on my back.

I had horseshoes put on, too. They felt stiff and heavy but I knew that they would protect my feet on the hard road.

Then my mother taught me to pull a carriage. "There are kind masters like ours," she said, "and there are cruel ones who should never have a horse. I hope you will have a kind master, but a horse never knows who will buy him."

Horseshoes
Iron horseshoes protect a horse's hooves from injury, especially when riding on hard roads or stones. A horse needs new shoes every few weeks.

Ginger and Merrylegs

Grooming
Grooming keeps
a horse clean.
Its face should
be groomed first.

Brushing
A soft body
brush is used
to clean and
smooth a
horse's coat
until it shines.

Soon, I had a new home with
Squire Gordon at Birtwick Park.
I met a little gray pony called
Merrylegs, and a tall chestnut mare
called Ginger. We became friends.

John Manly was the squire's
skilled coachman. When I arrived,
he gave me a good grooming. Then
the squire took me for a short ride.

"What shall we call this fine
horse?" the squire asked his wife
when we arrived home.

"He's certainly a beauty,"
Mrs. Gordon said, patting my nose.
"Let's call him Black Beauty."

I liked Birtwick Park. The only thing missing was freedom. As a grown-up horse, I stood in the stable when I wasn't working. It was a great treat when Ginger, Merrylegs, and I were let out into the old orchard. Then we ran across the soft grass or talked together under the shade of the big chestnut tree. Those were wonderful times!

Victorian horse stall
Stables were divided into stalls for each horse. Horses were taken out and exercised every day.

Danger warning
Horses have keen senses and can often foretell danger. They may rear if frightened.

One rainy day, I took Squire Gordon and John Manly to town. On the way, we had to stop at a tollgate before a low wooden bridge. The river was rising fast.

By the time we reached the bridge on the return trip, it was already dark. The moment I stepped on it, I knew something was wrong. I stopped and refused to go further.

John Manly tried to lead me across the bridge, but I wouldn't go.

Just then, the toll collector shouted, "The bridge is broken. You'll be swept downriver if you try to cross it."

"That was close," said John.

"I'm grateful that animals sense things that humans cannot know," said Squire Gordon in a quiet voice.

Horse listens to sounds from both directions

Moving ears
Horses can move their ears independently to pick up sounds more clearly from different directions.

Listening behind
The horse turns both ears back to listen to sounds from behind. It may do this when it's in a bad mood!

Danger at the inn

Room and board
Large coaching inns provided accommodation and food for travelers and their horses.

Stablehands
A stable boy mainly cleaned the stables and equipment.
A groom fed, groomed, and exercised the horses.

My master and his wife planned to visit friends some two days' drive away. We were to drive partway and stay overnight at an inn.

Ginger and I pulled the carriage and a stable boy called James drove us. James needed practice at driving in order to take up the offer of a job as a groom at another stable.

At the inn, an old hostler took charge of Ginger and me. James couldn't believe how quickly and thoroughly he cleaned me – my coat was as smooth as silk.

"I've had forty years practice looking after horses," the old hostler told James.

After he had gone, a second hostler came in with his friend.

The friend puffed on his pipe as he climbed up to the loft for some hay.

That night, I woke up to find the dark stable thick with smoke. I could hardly breathe. I heard Ginger coughing and the other horses moving about restlessly. They were neighing and stamping in fear. When I listened more closely, I could hear a low crackling noise. I didn't know what the noise was but it made me tremble all over.

Hostler
A hostler worked in the stables at a coaching inn. He would groom and feed the travelers' horses.

Horse sense
With its keen senses, a horse can even feel a fly on its tail. Imagine how sensitive a horse would be to a fire!

Fire!
Fire spreads quickly in wooden buildings like the stable.

At last, the second hostler came, but we wouldn't follow him. He was so frightened himself that he frightened the horses even more.

Then the old hostler arrived and began leading the horses. This time we followed, for he was gentle and firm. As I waited my turn, I saw flames spreading from the loft.

"Come, Beauty," said a quiet voice. It was James!

Quickly, he tied a scarf over my eyes.

He didn't want me to panic at the sight of the flames as he led me to safety. Then James raced back to the burning stable with his scarf. At last, I saw him lead Ginger away from the fire.

Firefighters
Firefighters wore metal helmets to protect their heads. They were often on duty for 100 hours a week.

I neighed with joy and relief. "You're a brave lad, James," the squire told him.

Just then two strong horses dashed into the yard pulling a fire engine behind them.

Fire engines
Fire engines were pulled by dapple-gray horses who could be seen in the dark.

Sleeping
Black Beauty
may have been
sleeping on
his feet when
John Manly
woke him.

The new stable boy

Of course, James got the job as groom at the other stable. I was glad for him.

Joe Green became the stable boy at Birtwick Park. Joe was only 14, but John Manly said he was a willing and kindhearted boy.

One night, John Manly woke me. "We must fetch Dr. White," he said. "Mrs. Gordon is very ill. Hurry!"

Away we went, across the grounds of Birtwick Park toward the town.

The air was frosty and the moon was bright. The doctor lived eight miles away and I galloped as fast as I could for every one of those miles.

"You're needed at Birtwick Park," John told the doctor as soon as we arrived. "Mrs. Gordon is very ill, sir."

Dr. White agreed to come, but his horses were not available.

"Black Beauty should have a rest after galloping all the way here," said John. He stroked my neck. I was very tired but I lifted my head high. I wanted the chance to help. "But I'm sure he'll do his best."

Indeed, I galloped all the way home at top speed. The doctor hurried to see the patient, while Joe Green led me to the stable. I have never been so glad to get home.

Horse paces
A horse has four basic paces – walk, trot, canter, and gallop.

Galloping
The rider leans forward to gallop. This is the fastest pace.

Horse blanket
After strenuous exercise, a horse should be kept warm with a blanket so it does not lose body heat.

Hot oats
Warm gruel, made from oats and water, is easy to digest after exercise.

I was so tired that my legs shook and I panted heavily. My coat was wet with sweat. Joe rubbed me down and gave me hay and corn with a pail of cold water. But after hard exercise, that was not what I needed.

Soon, I began to feel very cold and my body ached. Though he was tired after walking the eight miles home, John came straight to the stable. He covered me with my blanket and made me some warm gruel. By now I was very ill.

John nursed me and the squire came to see me too. "You saved your mistress' life, Beauty," he said.

I was very glad to hear that.

The horse doctor left some strong medicine for John to give to me. One night, Joe Green's father came to help John give me a dose.

"Joe did the best he knew," said Mr. Green. "He feels terrible."

"Ignorance is no excuse," John replied sharply.

The next morning, I felt better than I had in many days.

Joe Green learned quickly from his mistake and soon became a fine stable boy. In fact, I came to like him very much.

Horse doctor
A Victorian vet mainly treated working animals like horses.

Medicine
Medicine was poured through a hollow horn into a horse's mouth.

Galloping on

The Gordons moved abroad and could not take us with them. Merrylegs went to a family nearby. Ginger and I went to a new master at a grand estate called Earlshall.

Our new mistress liked to force her horses to hold their heads up high with a bearing rein. This was the very height of fashion. But it was very difficult for us to pull a carriage without being able to move our heads.

Fashion first
For the rich, fashion often took priority over comfort.

One day, our mistress told York, the coachman, to tighten the bearing rein as far as it would go. York protested but in the end, he did what he was told. He tightened my rein first. My head was in such an awkward position that I could only just endure it.

Then York took Ginger's rein off so he could tighten it. Ginger reared up, kicking so hard that she lost her balance and fell to the ground.

"Confound these bearing reins!" York muttered.

Once Ginger's bruises were better, one of the master's sons said that he would like to have her to ride. I was still put in the carriage with a tight bearing rein. How I hated it!

Bearing rein
A tight bearing rein forced the horse to hold its head up high in a very uncomfortable position.

Looser rein
A loose bearing rein gave a horse a little more freedom of movement. However, there was no real need for the bearing rein at all, except for the sake of fashion.

Sideways
Women wore long skirts and rode sidesaddle.

Pommel

Sidesaddle
The rider curved her leg around the pommel while sidesaddle.

One day, my master's daughter, Lady Anne, saddled a high-spirited mare called Lizzie. Her friend, a gentleman called Blantyre, put a saddle on me and we set off to deliver a message in the village.

Blantyre went to the door with the message. I was waiting with Lizzie and Lady Anne when a colt bolted past, brushing against Lizzie. Startled, she reared on her hind legs.

Lady Anne clung to the reins for a wild ride. I neighed loudly to get Blantyre's attention. Quickly, he jumped in the saddle and we dashed after them. Lizzie tried to jump over a high bank, but fell.

Luckily, I landed safely.

Rearing
Horses may rear before they bolt.

Lady Anne lay very still in the heather. Some local men ran to help and I took one of them to fetch the doctor.

A few days later, Blantyre told me that Lady Anne was not too badly hurt. I was glad to hear that she would be riding again soon.

Jumping
An experienced horse can judge the height and distance of a jump. The rider should also be in jumping position.

Fitting shoes
Blacksmiths fit horseshoes specially to each horse. The method of shoeing horses hasn't changed since Black Beauty's time.

Nails

Horseshoe

Pincers

Replacing horseshoes
The loose nail in Black Beauty's shoe should have been pulled out with pincers and then replaced.

While York was in London with my master, he left Reuben Smith in charge. Smith liked to drink, but so far had kept his promise not to drink another drop of alcohol. York trusted him.

But one day, Smith and I went into town, where he ran into some friends. He went with them to the tavern, leaving me at the stable.

When he finally came to collect me that evening, the stableman told him that I had a loose nail in one of my horseshoes.

"It'll do for now," Smith replied. He would have known better if he hadn't been drunk.

As I galloped over the stony road, my horseshoe came off. The sharp stones hurt my foot dreadfully. I lost my balance and stumbled. As I fell to my knees, Smith was thrown forward.

He hit the road with a thud and didn't move again.

Late in the night, two men arrived from Earlshall.

"Reuben is dead!" said one man.

"Look," said the other. "Beauty's knees are cut and his poor foot has no shoe. Reuben must have been drunk to ride on the road with a horseshoe missing."

If only Reuben had kept his promise to stay away from alcohol.

Injuries
A horse's feet and knees are the most easily injured parts of its body. Wounds must be cleaned and bandaged immediately to help healing.

Horse for sale

Gig
As a horse for rent, Black Beauty sometimes pulled a gig. A gig was easy to drive and only needed one horse.

Mucking out
Stables must be cleaned thoroughly every day. If a horse is kept in a dirty stable, its hooves can become infected.

My knees healed as well as possible. Then the Earl sold me to a man who rented out a horse and carriage to anyone who would pay. As a horse for rent, I experienced many different drivers. Some held the reins too tightly, others paid no attention to me or to the road. But when I was lucky enough to have a good driver, the ride was very pleasant.

Then I was sold to a new master, who hired a groom called Alfred Smirk to look after me. Alfred was vain and lazy. He never cleaned out the dirty straw in my stall but only covered it over with fresh straw. Soon, my stall began to smell and my feet became sore from standing on the filthy straw.

"Why has this horse become so clumsy?" asked my master.

"I don't know," Alfred replied.

Of course he hadn't noticed that Smirk rarely exercised me. I sometimes spent days standing in the dirty straw in my stall.

One day, my master took me for a ride and I stumbled quite badly. He took me to a horse doctor, who told him that my sore feet were the result of a dirty stall. From then on, my master made sure I was cared for properly until he could sell me.

Exercise
A horse should be able to stretch its legs every day with some exercise.

Horse auction
At auctions, horses were paraded in front of buyers from every walk of life.

I was taken to be sold at a horse auction. There were all kinds of horses for auction at the fair, and many kinds of buyers. The buyers checked my teeth and examined my body. But as soon as they saw the scars on my knees, nearly everyone turned away.

There was one man with gentle, gray eyes who seemed very kind. He made an offer of twenty-three pounds for me, but my salesman thought he could get more. Someone else offered the same but he did not look so kind.

As the fair drew to a close, my salesman was disappointed that he had not sold me.

To my delight, the man with the gray eyes came back. I reached out my head toward him and he stroked my face kindly.

"My name is Jerry," he said softly. "I think you and I are very well suited." He turned to my salesman. "I'll pay twenty-four pounds for him."

"Sold!" said my salesman.

Jerry gave me a good meal of oats and talked to me softly while I ate. Then we set off for London. We arrived in the big city just as the stars began to light up the night sky.

Light horse
Buyers wanted light horses, like Black Beauty, to pull carriages. Heavier horses made good farm horses.

Buying a horse
Certain places were regular sites for auctions, such as this one in North London.

Busy city
London streets were crowded with horse-drawn traffic.

Cab stands
There were 500 cab stands in London, where drivers waited for customers.

A city horse

It took me some time to get used to the noise and crowds of London, but I trusted Jerry completely. He was a cab driver and I was his cab horse. He only drove me hard if the customer had good reason.

One day, we saw a man fall on the cobblestones. Jerry ran to help him up. The man was dazed but not hurt.

"This fall has made me late. I mustn't miss the twelve o'clock train," he said. "Can you take me to the station?"

Jerry helped the man into the cab. "We'll do our best."

The roads were full of carriages, carts, wagons, and omnibuses. But Jerry expertly guided me through the traffic to the station.

"Thank you, sir, and your good horse," said the man. "Here is some extra money for you."

"Thank you, sir. I'm just glad we could help," said Jerry.

Growler
Jerry probably drove a cab like this one, called a "growler" after the sound the wheels made on roads.

One day, a shabby, old cab drove up beside ours to wait for a fare. The horse's bones showed plainly under her dull chestnut-colored coat; but somehow she looked familiar to me.

"Black Beauty, is that you?" she asked.

It was Ginger! But how much she had changed! Her lively spirit had been crushed by great suffering. She said that she had been sold several times, and each time her master had been cruel and worked her hard. Her health had got worse.

"You used to stand up for yourself if you were treated poorly," I said.

Cruelty
Horses had to pull all kinds of vehicles and were beaten if they were slow.

"There is nothing we can do if men want to be cruel," Ginger said sadly. "We can only bear it until the end. And I wish the end would come soon. I don't know how much longer I can bear the pain."

I put my nose up to Ginger's to comfort her, but just then, her driver tugged the rein at her mouth and they drove off.

A few weeks later, I saw a cart carrying a dead horse. It was a chestnut mare with a long thin neck. I thought it might be Ginger. I truly hoped it was my friend and that her troubles were now over.

It was Election Day and many people wanted cabs. A poor young woman, carrying a crying child, asked Jerry for directions to the nearest hospital.

"I will take you there for nothing," said Jerry.

The grateful woman began to climb into the cab.

Suddenly, two men pushed her aside. "We've got urgent election business," they declared.

"You will have to find another cab," said Jerry. "This one is taken."

Election Day
This was always very busy, as members of the political parties tried to persuade people to vote for their candidates.

Jerry refused to drive the men in his cab. They were angry but at last they left. Then we wove our way through the traffic to the hospital as quickly as we could.

"Thank you so much," said the woman, as she carried the crying child into the hospital building.

A moment later, another woman hailed the cab. "Jeremiah Barker, is that you?" she said. "What luck!"

"Mrs. Fowler, what a wonderful surprise!" Jerry replied.

As we drove Mrs. Fowler to the station, I learned that Jerry's wife used to work for her.

"If you ever get tired of cab work, I'll give you a job in the country," she said.

We left Mrs. Fowler at the station and drove home, tired after a very busy day.

London traffic Jerry took the woman to St. Thomas's Hospital, just south of the River Thames (TEMS). The Thames bridges were always teeming with traffic.

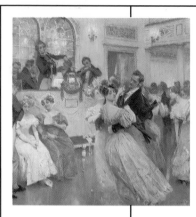

Party time
Rich Victorians held balls and parties during the time between Christmas and New Year.

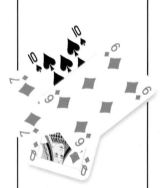

Card games
The Victorians liked to invite guests around to play cards. Such parties were called "at homes."

Despite Jerry's bad cough, we worked late into the cold winter nights during the Christmas season. On New Year's Eve, we took some gentlemen to a card party.

At nine o'clock, the party had not yet finished. We had to wait outside in the freezing wind and sleet.

Finally, at a quarter past one in the morning, the gentlemen finally appeared.

By then, Jerry's cough was really bad. But the gentlemen had the nerve to argue when Jerry charged for the time that we had waited for them.

The next day, Jerry was taken ill.

When the doctor told him that driving a cab was not good for his health, Jerry decided to accept Mrs. Fowler's offer of a job.

After three years as a cab horse, I had to be sold again. But I was not as strong as I had once been.

Tough life
A cab driver's life was a hard one. They were poorly paid and worked long hours. Some passengers expected them to wait for hours in the cold.

Corn dealer
A corn dealer traded in all types of grain, such as wheat and oats. He also baked and sold bread.

Cart horse
These were usually used by traders to pull carts. They were heavier and stronger than Beauty.

Hard times

Jerry sold me to a corn dealer and baker who was well respected. He thought I would be treated well. However, the corn dealer had a foreman called Jakes working for him who was not so sympathetic.

One day, I was trying with all my might to pull an extra-heavy cart up a hill when Jakes whipped me. To be punished when I was trying my best was quite unfair.

Just then, a lady approached Jakes. "There is no need to whip your horse," she told him in a quiet voice. "He is doing his best."

"His best isn't good enough if it won't move this load," Jakes replied, raising the whip again.

"Why don't you take off the bearing rein?" the lady suggested.

Jakes rolled his eyes but did as she asked. I tossed my head to relieve the stiffness in my neck.

Without the bearing rein, I could use my whole body to move the cart slowly but surely up the hill.

"You won't use the bearing rein again, will you?" said the lady.

"The horse does work better without it," Jakes admitted. "But the bearing rein is the fashion."

"It's better to lead a good fashion than to follow a bad one," the lady told Jakes. "Don't you agree?"

Hard work
Horses were used to pull all kinds of goods. Ponies like the one above hauled coal from the mines.

My next master owned a fleet of London cabs. Skinner worked his drivers hard and my driver worked me harder, using his whip where it hurt most. I began to wish that my suffering might end as Ginger's had.

One hot summer day, my driver and I picked up a family with a great deal of luggage.

"Papa, this is too much for the horse to take," said the little girl.

My driver wanted a large tip so he insisted that we could take it all. The carriage was loaded up and we started on our way.

I struggled up the hill towards St Paul's Cathedral. I felt the painful crack of the whip, but I could go on no further. I fell to the ground and could not move.

Luggage
Cabs were allowed up to six passengers, but there was no limit to the amount of luggage they could carry.

"This horse hasn't much strength left," the horse doctor told Skinner.

"I can't use a sick horse," Skinner snapped. "He would be better off dead."

"If you rest him and feed him well, someone may buy him at a horse sale," said the doctor.

Luckily, Skinner agreed. After some rest and good food, I felt that life was worth living again.

On the beat
The police could fine the owners if horses blocked roads.

Star
The markings on a horse's head have names. Beauty has a "star."

Blaze
This horse has a "star and stripe" between the eyes.

My golden years

At the next horse sale, a boy took a liking to me. "Grandpapa, will you buy this horse and make him young again?" he asked.

"I suppose we can try, Willie," he replied, to his grandson's delight.

They brought me to their farm, where I could rest or run in the meadow as I pleased.

"He's growing young, Willie," the boy's grandfather remarked.

He found me a home with three kind young ladies who doted on me.

My new groom looked at me closely. "You have a star on your forehead just like Black Beauty." He looked me in the eye.

Then he smiled.

"Beauty, it is you, isn't it? Do you remember me? I'm little Joe Green."

I did not recognize Joe at first. He had grown from a young boy into a fine young man.

"I can see you've had some hard times, Beauty," said Joe. "But I'll make sure that you only have good times now. Your troubles are over."

Joe was right – finally my troubles are over. He is the best and kindest of grooms and my mistresses have said that they will never sell me. At last, I am truly at home.

At last, I am truly at home.

A fine friend
With lots of love and proper care, an older horse can live a happy, healthy life.

Anna Sewell

Anna Sewell
At times, Anna was so ill that she had to tell Black Beauty's story to her mother, who wrote it down for her.

Bearing rein
Horses in bearing reins came to carry Anna's coffin at her funeral – her mother demanded they be removed.

The author of *Black Beauty* was born in 1820 and grew up in London. She loved horses from an early age, often visiting her uncle's farm where she greatly enjoyed riding. Her eager interest in horses continued throughout her life.

Anna Sewell wrote *Black Beauty* while plagued by ill-health. She died in 1878, a year after it was published.

But her book had a lasting impact on the campaign for better treatment of horses. In 1914, the bearing rein on horse-drawn vehicles was finally banned, one of Anna Sewell's dearest wishes.

The book has never been out of print. Even though we now only use horses for sports and leisure, Beauty's voice continues to teach young readers to treat horses with respect.

Keeping watch
Black Beauty was an instant hit. Millions of children who read it learned that horses had strong feelings.

Glossary

Autobiography
The story of a person's life, written by that person.

Bearing rein
A rein that runs from the horse's mouthpiece to the saddle, designed to keep the horse's head in a high position. Horses found bearing reins uncomfortable.

Bridle
The headgear for a horse, consisting of a set of buckled straps and a metal mouthpiece. The bridle helps to control and guide the horse.

Campaign
A series of planned actions that are organized to achieve a particular goal.

Coachman
The person who drives a horse-drawn coach or carriage.

Colt
A young male horse or similar animal, including a donkey and a zebra.

Election
The process of voting for a person or persons from among candidates, usually to form a government.

Endure
To keep going and put up with terrible strain or pain.

Estate
The land belonging to a wealthy family in the countryside. Estates are made up of houses, gardens, and farms.

Equine
Relating to, or looking like, a horse. Belonging to the horse family.

Gallop
A word used to describe how a horse or other four-legged creature runs. A galloping horse lifts all four feet off the ground at one time while it is running as fast as it can.

Groom
A person who is employed to clean and look after horses.

Hostler
The person in charge of the stables at an inn. The word is no longer generally used.

Mare
An adult, female horse or zebra.

Omnibus
The full word for "bus", which is no longer used.

Pony
A type of small horse.

Saddle
A seat for a rider, which is usually made of leather. A saddle is fastened undereath a horse's belly.

Tollgate
A gate at which a toll is collected. A toll is a charge for using a road or bridge. Tolls are taken from travelers by toll collectors.

Sympathetic
Someone who feels sorry for another's suffering, or shares another's feelings as if they were his or her own.

Victorian
Something that happened in Britain during the reign of Queen Victoria (1837–1901).